Alfonso Grambone

The Grove Dogs

Bumblebee Books
London

A CIP catalogue record for this title is
available from the British Library.

ISBN: 978-1-83934-564-7

Bumblebee Books is an imprint of
Olympia Publishers.

First Published in 2023

Bumblebee Books
Tallis House
2 Tallis Street
London
EC4Y 0AB

Printed in Great Britain

www.olympiapublishers.com

Acknowledgements

I would like to thank my wife, Michelle, for her ongoing support and assistance in writing and editing my work. I would also like to thank my friends and family for inspiring me and helping me bring my characters to life. To my niece, Julianna, thank you for being my biggest inspiration for wanting me to create a children's book. To my nephews, Nicholas, Alex, Matteo, and Adrian, thank you for helping me capture the innocence of childhood and the simplicities of life. Lastly, but certainly not least, I need to thank my dogs, Harley and Grayson, for being two of the most faithful and loyal friends anyone could ask for.

Alfie can hear the pitter-patter of padded feet as Harley made her way down the hall and into his bedroom. She entered carrying her favorite chew toy, a rubber pig that oinked as she chewed it. She dropped her chew toy and licked Alfie's face before plopping down in bed for a good night's sleep.

Harley is a very happy bulldog and she is Alfie's best friend. Alfie rested his hands behind his head as he lay in bed staring at the ceiling remembering the day he and Harley met.

The story begins about a year ago. Harley was born on a potato farm with her brother and sister. There was just too many puppies for the little old farmer and his wife to care for, so he arranged to send the puppies to a pet store in Paterson Grove so they can find loving new homes. Harley doesn't remember much about life on the farm except the day she had to leave. When she was only three months old, she and her siblings were placed in a crate and put in a truck. As the truck drove off she could see the farmhouse getting smaller until she could no longer see it. The truck continued along the winding dirt road which seemed to go on for miles.

While en route, the truck hit a bump in the road so hard it caused a flat tire. The truck began to slow down, and the driver pulled over to the side of the road.

As the driver was getting the spare tire he bumped into the crate of puppies and the door popped open. All three puppies scampered out of the crate and jumped out of the truck.

The driver scrambled to gather the puppies, but was only able to catch two. Harley wandered off the road, passing a sign that read 'Welcome to Paterson Grove'. As she made her way through the bushes, deep in the grove, she realized she was lost, all alone, and very far from home.

On the other side of town Alfie was busy getting ready for school. He quickly got dressed, ran downstairs to the kitchen, and began to fill his lunch box with snacks before his mother noticed.

"Alfie! Alfie! Hey, Alfie!" Brian stood outside on the front lawn calling for Alfie in anticipation for their first day of school. Alfie quickly closed his lunch box and made his way to the front door.

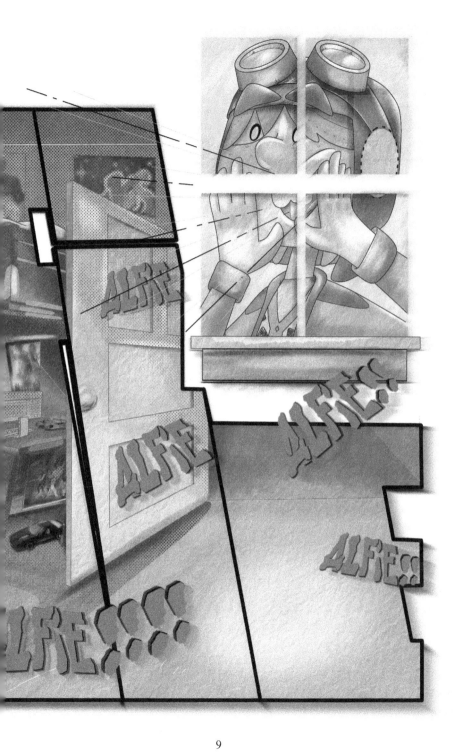

His mother was waiting for him at the door with open arms. She gave him a big hug and an even bigger kiss on the cheek. "Have a good day and tell Brian to use the doorbell next time."

"OK, Mom," Alfie replied as he grabbed his book bag and wiped his cheek hoping Brian didn't see. He waved goodbye to his mother as he ran out the front door.

"Hurry, Alfie, we have to meet Pete and Sandy at their house."

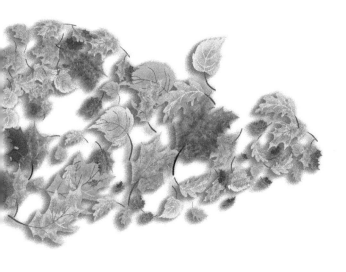

As they made their way to Pete's house, Alfie asked Brian if he ever found the baseball he lost during their game last week. "No," replied Brian. "That was the third one I lost this summer. Sandy even helped me look because she lost five balls."

"That's strange," said Alfie. "We know they were hit into the grove. They couldn't have just disappeared."

They continued to walk down one more block before Brian stopped on the front lawn and began shouting, "Pete! Pete!" Alfie put his hand over Brian's mouth muffling his shouts.

He then continued up the front steps and rang the doorbell. Alfie was greeted by Pete's mom and was told Pete and Sandy would be out in just a minute.

Down in the basement, Pete was finishing up his latest invention. "Just one more screw and it should work," he said.

Sandy just shook her head. "Mom is not going to be happy when she sees you took apart the vacuum cleaner. Especially since it's your week to do the chores," replied Sandy.

Their conversation was interrupted by their mother who was calling them from the top of the stairs. "Alfie and Brian must be here. Get your bookbag. We have to go," Pete said to Sandy. The two children hurried up the stairs, kissed their mother goodbye, and ran out the door.

The four children arrived at Mrs. Clark's classroom just in time. The school bell rang as they each made their way to their desks. As Mrs. Clark began roll call, Brian leaned

over and whispered to Alfie, "Has anyone seen Vincent since he returned from his camping trip with the boy scouts?" Alfie pointed to the back of the classroom.

Vincent climbed up a tree, grabbed onto the drain pipe, and scaled across the window ledge until he reached the opened window. This is the type of sneak entrance Vincent wishes he could pull off. He was actually standing by the backdoor of the classroom peeking in. He spotted an empty desk and army crawled his way to his seat without the teacher noticing. Brian slipped Vincent a note that read, 'Meet us at the baseball field after school'.

The time was 2:55pm and Mrs. Clark's class was gathering the books they needed for homework and proceeded to line up by the door waiting for the dismissal bell to ring.

At the sound of the final bell, Alfie, Brian, Pete, Sandy and Vincent made their way over to the baseball field. As they walked past second base, Brian reached into his book bag and pulled out a baseball. He got into wind-up position and threw a fastball over the fence. "What did you do that for?" asked Vincent.

"Just keep your eye on the ball," said Brian. "We are about to crack the case of the missing baseballs."

"Crack it fast," said Alfie. "Mr Doughnut is about to put out the late afternoon batch of sugar crawlers."

"Oh give your belly a break. This is more important," Brian exclaimed. The crew made their way through the gate of the back fence to retrieve the ball.

"Pete, did you hear that?" asked Sandy. "Something is moving over there," she said as she pointed toward the bushes.

"And the ball is gone!" shouted Vincent.

"What the heck was that? We need to go after it!" Brian said with a sense of urgency.

"Are you crazy?" asked Alfie. "Do you even know what goes on in the grove. I heard a boy went in there to go fishing and he never came out. And besides that, I'm always hearing strange noises coming from the grove late at night."

"That is why we need to work together," said Sandy. "Why don't we meet at Alfie's house Saturday morning and enter the grove from the other end," she suggested.

"That's a great idea! And we can sneak up behind whatever THAT was and get our baseballs back," Brian said with excitement.

Afie pulled opened the curtains to his bedroom window hoping for a rainy Saturday afternoon. Of course, with Alfie's luck, the sun was shining and there was not a single cloud in the sky. Ding dong! Ding dong! Alfie froze in a panic wondering how he was going to get out of going to the grove. He quickly wrapped a blanket around his body and made his way to the door. "Hi, guys," he moaned, "I'm not feeling well. I think I'll stay behind and get some rest."

"You're going," Sandy said, as she grabbed him by the arm and pulled him out the door.

The gang stood just outside the grove strategizing the best way to head in and get out with their baseballs. Brian took a few steps closer. "Sandy and I should go in first. I have my slingshot and she brought her baseball bat."

"I brought a first aid kit in case of an emergency," said Vincent.

"And I have my junior detective forensic kit," said Pete.

"What did you bring Alfie?" asked Brian.

"I brought snacks in case we get hungry," he answered.

"Great! We can use your snacks to make a trail so we don't get lost," said Brian.

They began to make their way deep into the grove. There was no real trail to follow, only Alfie's fruit snack trail.

They were surrounded by trees as they approached a moss-covered lake. "Look," said Sandy as she pointed in the distance. "There is the old church that burned down during the town festival years ago. We must be close to the baseball field now." Just beyond the building was the junkyard. There was crushed cars stacked on top of each other and piles of burnt tires.

As they got closer to the church, they began to hear the rustling of leaves. It was coming from inside the remaining walls of the church. With the roof completely gone, they were able to see inside although they couldn't quite make out what was there. Vincent was a few feet ahead of the rest and was able to get a better view.

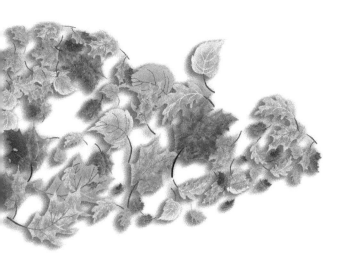

From under the leaves he could see a set of eyes staring right back at him. The creature stood up and began to shake off the leaves. Just as it was about to lunge toward them Vincent began to shout, "It's a mutated mud monster! Run!" He turned around and began to follow Alfie's trail out of the grove. The crew quickly followed as Alfie trailed slightly behind.

"Hurry, Alfie! Hurry! It's gaining on you," shouted Brian as he looked over his shoulder. Alfie started slowing down in an attempt to catch his breath. At that moment the mutated mud monster leaped up and grabbed hold of Alfie's backpack.

"It's got me! It's got me!" he shouted as he fell to his knees.

"Take off your backpack," said Brian, "it wants your food."

"No!" replied Alfie. "I have a number five from Phil's Atomic Hero Deli." Brian ran back toward Alfie, pulled off his backpack and helped him to his feet as they continued to run out of the grove. The mutated mud monster dragged Alfie's backpack all the way back to the leaf pile inside the abandoned church and began to feast on a number five from the Atomic Hero menu.

On the walk home Vincent was the first to announce their need for a plan of attack. "Are you crazy?" asked Alfie. "He nearly took my head off and he took my lunch. My seasoned steak with melted provolone and fresh onions and pickles and that delicious buttered bun. I can't handle another loss that big. I won't go back," he proclaimed.

"Wait a minute," said Pete. "We know the mud monster likes baseballs, right? and we know he likes number five's."

"So what's your point?" asked Brian.

"I am glad you asked," said Pete. "I've been working on an invention that I think I could use to distract the muddy beast while you all collect the baseballs."

"And whatever's left of Alfie's buttery buns," Brian added.

"Let's all agree to meet at my house next Saturday morning," said Pete.

"Agreed," they all said in unison.

One week later the whole crew gathered at Pete and Sandy's house. Pete led them into the garage where he kept his latest invention hidden under an old sheet. "I give you the mud monster 3000," he said as he pulled off the sheet for the big reveal.

"How is this suppose to help us?" asked Alfie.

"It's part vacuum, part baseball pitching machine, and part food dispenser. After rummaging through the garage and making several trips to the grocery store, I think I have everything we will need. Now let's take back what's ours," Pete said with determination.

The gang walked very cautiously through the grove. Alfie made sure to stay in the middle of the pack this time. "We can still turn around and go back," he suggested. "We can go to 'Corkey's Pigs' and get hot dogs. My treat."

"How can you think of food at a time like this?" asked Vincent. "We have to complete our mission." They walked a little further until they were close enough to see inside the abandoned church.

"I don't see anything," said Sandy.

"Let me turn on the mud monster 3000 and maybe it'll come out," said Pete. "Everyone stand back." He pushed the button on the side and waited for his device to warm up.

"That sure is loud," said Brian.

"It's not suppose to make that noise," said Pete. "I hope it's not broken."

"Oh no! Look over there," said Sandy as she pointed in the distance. The noise they were hearing was the sound of dirt bikes heading toward them.

"Great," said Alfie, "it's Nick and his friends. They are so mean, can we go now?" he asked. Before anyone had time to answer him they were surrounded by three dirt bikes.

"What are you all doing here?" said Nick. He got off his bike and took off his helmet. "Don't you know the grove is our hang out?"

"We are not here to hang out," said Brian. "We just came to collect our missing baseballs."

Nick, who had to be about a foot taller than Brian, pushed Brian out of the way and walked toward Alfie. He grabbed the backpack from his shoulder. "What do you have here, fatso."

"I'm not fat, I'm husky," Alfie replied.

Nick unzipped the backpack. "Hey look, guys, a number five, my favorite." Alfie took a few steps back, but not in fear of Nick and his friends, but rather what was standing behind him. The sound of a deep growl caused Nick to turn around. With a frightened look he held out his arms to hold back the creature as it lunged at him. The mud monster knocked him down and took the number five from his hand. Nick quickly ran back to his bike and the three bikes rode off.

"And don't come back!" shouted Alfie.

The gang turned their attention back to the mysterious creature, "It's not a mud monster," said Sandy with a laugh. "It's just a puppy."

"Who is in desperate need of a bath," added Brian. The puppy led the group into the church where she was hiding their baseballs. They immediately fell in love with the lost dog as they watched her feast on Alfie's lunch.

"Now that we've solved the mystery we should head back home. It's getting late," said Vincent. They gathered up their things and headed out of the church. Alfie looked back to wave goodbye to the puppy only to notice that she was standing by his side.

"You have to stay," said Alfie, as he took a few steps back. The dog stayed as Alfie took a few more steps, but then she began to follow him. "Stay," Alfie repeated. The dog stopped for a moment and then jumped up into Alfie's arms and licked his face.

"Looks like you made a new friend," said Brian.

"And we don't leave friends behind," said Alfie. "Let's go, buddy. Your gonna come live with me now." The gang left the grove with the puppy by their side. From that day forward they called themselves the Grove Dogs.

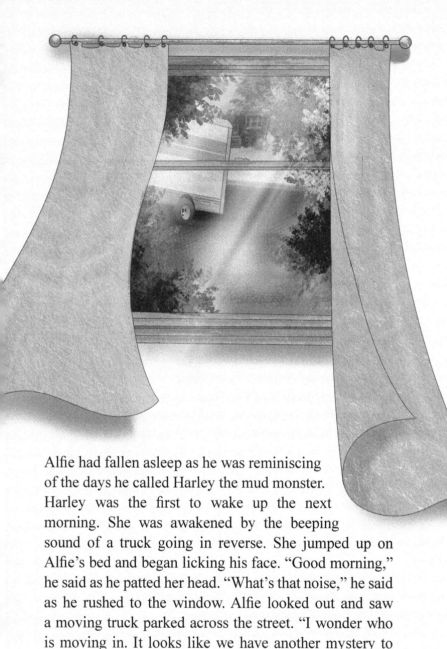

Alfie had fallen asleep as he was reminiscing of the days he called Harley the mud monster. Harley was the first to wake up the next morning. She was awakened by the beeping sound of a truck going in reverse. She jumped up on Alfie's bed and began licking his face. "Good morning," he said as he patted her head. "What's that noise," he said as he rushed to the window. Alfie looked out and saw a moving truck parked across the street. "I wonder who is moving in. It looks like we have another mystery to solve," he said to Harley.

About the Author

Alfonso Grambone was born and brought up in Paterson, New Jersey. His mother, Josephine, and father, Vincenzo, met and married in the U.S. emigrating from Italy. Alfonso's earlist illustration was of Pac-Man he copied from his Pac-Man cereal box. He continued to improve his talent by drawing cartoon characters for his classmates, including He-man, Shera, and Voltron and many more. His inspiration was to write a children's book after the birth of his eldest niece, Julianna. It wasn't until he met his wife, Michelle, that his dream became a reality. Michelle's experience in journalism helped Alfonso develop the Grove Dogs.

CPSIA information can be obtained
at www.ICGtesting.com
Printed in the USA
BVHW012308220123
656879BV00021B/1189